"I would do it
because I love you."

"Wow, I'm somebody!"

the Little Soul shouted,
"I'm the Light!"

"I can be as special as I want to be!"

小靈魂與太陽

The Little Soul and the Sun

（中英雙語版）

尼爾·唐納·沃許◎著　法蘭克·瑞奇歐◎圖

劉美欽◎譯

這本好看的書會讓人變得更好看

暢銷書《好笑華娟撞見維也納咖啡》作者　鄭華娟

　　如果你正在找一本好看的書，我想你一定要看這一本，因為我反覆讀了好幾遍，只覺得越來越好看，而且不是越讀越瞭解這位作者和這個故事，反而是更完整地認識自己！好看的書才有這樣的魔力，照見你的面容，深入你的心。

　　我看完這個小故事高興地哭了。我當然是有點容易被感動、愛流淚啦，不過當我發現自己原來是很特殊的人，不是自己誤認的那樣平凡時，我是又驚訝又高興！我？很特別？真的！你？也很特別！一點不假喔！我一直以為特別的人是那種很厲害的成功人士，就是以一般社會的標準所認定的超優秀人物，可是我們卻忽略了自己，將自己的特別遺忘了，更糟的是，根本不知自己很特別，也沒有人告訴你，真是太可惜了。

　　這本好看的書除了說明我們每個人都很特別之外，還說連我們討厭的人也很特別！哇，這起先真讓我難以接受！不相信吧？當提起讓我們心煩意亂的人時，可能總會想：「唉，要是生命中沒這號人物就好了，還特別哩，我看是特別煩吧……」但這本書告訴我們一個美麗的秘密，這個秘密會讓我們重新評價那個討厭的人，就在這一刻，討厭的人竟然讓我們的性情更完善平和，那個討厭的人正是我們上個生命周期中約好來相會的天使哩！從來沒想過吧？這本書真的會讓你重新檢視一遍目前的生活，發現你本來就會發熱發光的心，已經好久沒有擦拭一下了；這本好看的書會讓你變成好看的人。

看完這本書，發現成為快樂和成熟的自己其實好簡單！幼稚悲愁的人總期待著被忍耐、被理解和被寬恕，而真正認識自己的人總是滿心充滿著忍耐、理解和寬恕，這其中只差一個「被」字就差很多！我以前都沒想過是這樣呀，你呢？

「認識自己」是人生中最美也最該努力的事，期望你讀了這個有趣的故事會從此將曾遺忘了的那特別的自己找回來，你會明白我為什麼說這本好看的書會讓人變得更好看。

加油！讓我們一起努力地「認識自己」！

黑暗中的亮光

國家文藝獎終身成就獎得主　林良

只有在黑暗中做「亮光」，才能體會做「亮光」的滋味，才能成為真正的「亮光」。

——這就是這本書想告訴你的一個感人的人生哲理。

中文世界缺乏的思考故事

兒童文學研究者、財團法人毛毛蟲兒童哲學基金會
創辦人 楊茂秀

這是一本對話精采的圖畫書。

從實相呈現出來的思考軌跡，含藏著最基本、最普遍的終極關懷，大人、小孩都會關心和會喜歡這個中文世界很缺乏的思考故事（Thinking Story）。

它值得養育小孩的人認真去體會，而且最好設法從孩子的反應中吸取一些心得。

喚起你我心中久遠的記憶

《與神同心》作者　王季慶

　　每個人，不論年齡，是否心中都藏著一個小小人兒，那就是，在童年時的夏夜，仰望星空，探入點點明星背後深邃的黑暗，喃喃自語：「很久很久以前……」的內在小孩？

　　沒錯，很久很久以前，不止是今生，還回溯到……你依稀記得，曾經……

不知道這本小小童書，多小的孩子便能懂。不過，我們心中那無年紀的，卻被觸動了。它試圖喚起的，可是每個人心中亙古的記憶。

　　當你面對外界，彷彿盡力阻撓你一切進展的人，彷彿全然漠視你的存在的人，彷彿否定你任何價值的人……你心中哭喊「為什麼」時；

　　當你躲在內心角落裡舔傷，當你恨自己因怨而扭曲變形的心靈，當你因不知如何寬恕別人而寬恕自己時；

　　當你飢寒交迫，孤苦無依，為世人遺忘時；

　　當你豐衣足食、功成名就，內心卻莫名地飢寒交迫時；

　　請憶起，小小蠟燭的故事。

　　請憶起，很久很久以前……

獻給我未來的孫兒，

以及每一個等待出世的小靈魂。

你們將擁有我們的祝福

與我們的期待，

我們的純真與我們的喜樂，

我們的承諾

和我們所見證的神的永恆之愛。

　　　　　——尼爾·唐納·沃許

獻給所有眩目的光。

　　　　　——法蘭克·瑞奇歐

很久很久以前，有一個小靈魂，他對神說：

「我知道我是誰了！」

於是，神說：「那真是太好了！那麼你是誰呢？」

小靈魂大聲地說：「我是光啊！」

神大笑了起來，並大聲地說：「沒錯！你就是光。」

小靈魂覺得非常高興，因為他為神的國度裡所有還在尋找答案的靈魂找到了答案。「哇，這真是太好了！」

但是很快地，小靈魂覺得知道自己是誰還不夠，他的內心有些激動，現在，他想「是」自己。於是，小靈魂來到神的身邊，他說：「嗨，神！現在，我知道我是誰了，那麼我可不可以是自己呢？」

　　於是神說：「你的意思是，你想是『已經是的你』嗎？」

　　「嗯，」小靈魂回答，「知道自己是誰是一回事；是真正的自己又是另一回事。我想感覺一下『光』到底像什麼？」

　　「但是，你已經是光了。」神一邊重複，一邊又笑了起來。

　　「沒錯。但是，我想知道那感覺像什麼。」小靈魂大聲說著。

　　「嗯，」神咯咯地笑著說，「我早該知道你總是喜歡冒險了。」然後，神的表情變了：「只是有一件事……」

　　「什麼事？」小靈魂問道。

「嗯，除了光以外，什麼都沒有。你明白嗎？除了你以外，我沒有創造出任何東西。所以，沒有什麼簡單的方法可以讓你親身體驗你是誰，因為沒有什麼是你不是的。」

「喔？」小靈魂應了一聲，他現在感到有點兒困惑了。

「這麼想吧，」神說，「你就像是太陽中的一根蠟燭，你在那兒好好的，跟其他數不清的蠟燭組成了太陽。但若少了你，太陽就不是原來的太陽了。

「哦，不，如果太陽少了其中一根蠟燭，它還是太陽……卻已經不是原先的太陽了，因為它的光不再那麼明亮。但當你在光裡，你怎麼知道自己是光呢？這就是問題的所在。」

小靈魂精神為之一振地說：「你是神，你想想看吧！」

神又笑了起來，「我已經知道了。好吧，既然當你身處在光當中，就看不見同樣是光的自己，那麼，我們就讓黑暗包圍你。」

「黑暗是什麼呢？」小靈魂問。

神回答說：「黑暗是你所不是的。」

「我會怕黑暗嗎？」小靈魂大聲地說。

「只有當你選擇害怕時才會。」神回答道。「說真的，沒有一樣東西會讓人害怕，除非你決定要如此。你明白嗎？一切都由我們來決定，都由我們來取決的。」

「喔。」小靈魂應了一聲，覺得比較舒服了。

然後，神解釋為了能體驗每一件事，所有事情的相反面便將呈現出來。「這是個很棒的禮物。」神說，「因為沒有它，你就不能明瞭任何事了。

「沒有冷，你就不能知道暖；沒有下，就不能知道上；沒有快，就不能知道慢；沒有左，你就不能知道右；沒有這兒，就不能知道那兒；沒有現在，就不能知道未來。

「所以，」神總結道，「當你被黑暗圍繞時，不要揮舞你的拳頭，或提高音量去咒罵它。

「你寧可成為黑暗前的光，也不要對它生氣。然後，你將知道你真正是誰，其他所有的靈魂也將知道。讓你的光燦爛無比，以致沒有一個靈魂不知道你是多麼地特別！」

「你是說，讓其他靈魂明白我多麼特別，是很好的嗎？」小靈魂問道。

「當然！」神低聲輕笑地說，「而且非常好！但是你要記住，『特別』不意味著『比較好』。每一個生命都是特別的，都有他們自己的特色！但是，很多的生命早已忘了這回事。只有當你明白你的特別是不錯時，他們才會明瞭，他們的特別是好的。」

「喔，」小靈魂跳著舞、活蹦亂跳地大笑起來說，「我可以像我想要的那樣特別！」

「是的，你可以從現在開始。」神說，他正陪著小靈魂一起跳著、舞著，並開懷大笑。「你想成為『特別』的哪一個部分呢？」

「『特別』的哪一個部分？」小靈魂重複地說，「我不懂。」

「嗯，」神解釋說，「成為光就是一件特別的事情，『特別』包含了很多的部分。和善是特別的、有風度是特別的、具有創造力是特別的、有耐心是特別的。你可以想到變得特別的其他方法嗎？」小靈魂靜靜地坐了一會兒，然後說：「我可以想到很多變得特別的方法！」小靈魂提高音量說：「熱心助人是特別的、與人分享是特別的、友好是特別的、善解人意是特別的！」

「沒錯！」神同意地說，「那些事情你全都可以去做，或者你也可以在任何時刻、做任何你希望成為特別的那個部分。這就是成為光的意思。」

「我知道我想成為什麼了，我知道我想成為什麼了！」小靈魂興奮無比地說，「我想成為『特別』的部分，叫做『寬恕』。寬恕難道不特別嗎？」

　　「喔，沒錯，」神向小靈魂保證，「那是非常特別的。」

　　「好，」小靈魂說，「那就是我想成為的。我想學著寬恕別人，我想親身體驗那種感覺。」

　　「很好，」神說，「但是，有一件事情，你應該知道。」

　　小靈魂現在變得有點兒不耐煩起來，事情總是比看起來的樣子複雜一些。「是什麼事情呢？」小靈魂嘆了一口氣。

　　「沒有人是要被寬恕的。」

　　「沒有人？」小靈魂幾乎不能相信他所聽到的話。

　　「沒有人！」神重複地說，「我做的所有事物都是完美的。在所有創造物中，沒有哪一個靈魂比你來得不完美。看看你的身旁。」

此時，小靈魂發現一大群靈魂已經聚了過來。他們從神的國度的四面八方長途跋涉來到這裡，就是為了小靈魂與神的這場精采對話，每個人都想聽聽他們在說什麼。

　　看到不計其數、聚在那裡的靈魂後，小靈魂必須同意神的話。沒有人比小靈魂還不精采、還不高貴，或是還不完美。小靈魂對聚在身旁的靈魂感到萬分訝異，他們的光多麼亮啊，以至於他幾乎不能直視他們。

　　「那麼，有誰是要被寬恕的呢？」神問。

　　「哎呀，這樣下去一點兒也不好玩！」小靈魂埋怨地說，「我想親身體驗做一個寬恕別人的人的感覺，我想知道特別的那個部分感覺像是什麼。」

　　這時，小靈魂體認到一種感覺，他想那一定就是悲傷了。

　　但是過了沒多久，友善的靈魂從人群中走了出來。

　　「小靈魂，不要擔心，」友善的靈魂說，「我可以幫助你。」

　　「是嗎？」小靈魂的心情開朗了起來。「但是你可以做什麼呢？」

　　「為什麼這麼問呢？我可以給你一個要被寬恕的人啊！」

　　「你可以嗎？」

　　「當然可以！」友善的靈魂輕快地說，「我可以進到你下一個生命期當中，為你做一些要被寬恕的事情。」

「但是，為什麼呢？為什麼你要那麼做呢？」小靈魂問，
「你，是一個那麼高尚完美的生命！你，振動得那麼快速，
快到可以創造出明亮的光，讓我幾乎不能直視你。是什麼力
量，使你想把你振動的速度放慢到你的光變得暗沉沉的？是
什麼力量，讓如此一個輕快到可以隨心所欲在星星上跳舞、
在神的國度裡四處穿梭的你，來到我的生命當中，並使你自
己變得如此沉重，而去做這麼糟糕的事情呢？」

　　「很簡單，」友善的靈魂說，「我願意這麼做，因為我愛
你。」

小靈魂似乎對這個回答感到非常驚訝。

　　「不要那麼吃驚嘛，」友善的靈魂說，「你曾為我做了同樣的事情，不記得了嗎？你跟我，我們一起共舞很多次了。我們一起共舞了好幾個年代，穿越時空，我們無時無地不在一起遊玩，只是你不記得了。

　　「我們兩個一股腦兒地跳，一上一下地跳，一左一右地跳；我們這兒跳跳，那兒跳跳；現在跳，等會兒跳。我們一個是男，一個是女；一個良善，一個邪惡──我們兩個，一個是受害者，一個是加害者。

　　「因此，你跟我，過去有好幾次在一起。我們都給過彼此完美、適當的機會，去表達、體驗我們真正是誰。

　　「因此，」友善的靈魂進一步解釋，「我將進入你的下一個生命期當中，這一次，我要去當一個『壞人』。我將做出真正可怕的事情，然後，你就可以親身體驗做一個寬恕別人的人是什麼感覺了。」

「但是，你將做出什麼事情呢？」小靈魂有點兒緊張地問，
「有那麼可怕嗎？」

「喔，」友善的靈魂眼睛閃閃發光地回答，「我們會想出
辦法的。」

然後，友善的靈魂似乎變得嚴肅起來，並冷靜地說：「你
知道，有件事情你是對的。」

「什麼事情啊？」小靈魂想要知道。

「我將放慢自己振動的速度，讓自己變得非常沉重，沉重
到可以去做這件不好的事情；我必須假扮成不像自己的樣子。
然後，我只請求你回頭幫我一個忙。」

「喔，什麼忙都可以！什麼忙都可以！」小靈魂大聲喊著，
同時又跳又唱了起來。「我要去寬恕別人，我要去寬恕別
人！」然後，小靈魂看到友善的靈魂整個人都沉默了下來。

「是什麼忙呢？」小靈魂問道，「我可以為你做些什麼嗎？
你是一個這麼願意為我付出的天使！」

「當然，友善的靈魂本來就是個天使啊！」神打岔道，「每一個人都是！你要永遠記得：我派遣給你的，都是天使。」

所以，小靈魂更加願意答應友善靈魂的請求。「我可以為你做什麼呢？」他又問了一次。

「當我攻擊你、打你的時候，」友善的靈魂回答，「當我對你做了你可能想像得到的最糟糕的事情時——就在那個非常的時刻裡……」

「嗯？」小靈魂打岔說，「然後呢？」

友善的靈魂變得更加沉默了。

「請記得我真正是誰。」

「喔，我會的。」小靈魂大喊著，「我答應！我會永遠記得：我就是在這個地方、這個時候看到你的！」

「很好，」友善的靈魂說，「因為，你知道，我必須辛苦地假裝，好忘了自己是誰。如果你不記得我真正是誰的話，我自己可能也會有很長一段時間不能記得。如果我忘了我是誰，你可能也會忘了你是誰，我們兩個都會迷失了方向。然後，我們需要另一個靈魂來到我們身旁，提醒我們兩個，我們是誰。」

　　「不，我們不會忘記的！」小靈魂再一次承諾，「我會記得你的！我將謝謝你帶給我這個禮物──這個親身體驗我是誰的機會。」

所以，協議達成了。小靈魂進到一個新的生命期當中，並興奮地成為非常特別的光，興奮地成為那個「特別」的部分——寬恕。

　　小靈魂不安地等待能夠親身經歷所謂的「寬恕」，並感謝讓這件事成為可能的其他靈魂所做的一切。

　　於是，在那個新生命期的每一個時刻裡，每當一個新的靈魂出現在舞台上，不管那個新的靈魂帶來的是歡樂，還是悲傷——尤其如果他帶來的是悲傷的話——小靈魂就會想起神曾經說過的話。

　　「你要永遠記得，」神微笑地說，「我派遣給你的，都是天使。」

給親愛的父母和所有喜愛孩子的人

這個精采的故事讓孩子們對於為什麼有時候會有「壞的」事情發生,有一個新的看法;也讓孩子們知道,當這些事情發生時,該如何處理。

這個故事還教導我們:「認為自己是特別的,並讓別人知道我們有多麼特別」,是一件非常好的事情。

最後,故事還告訴我們,神對每個人的愛都是一樣的,即使我們不認為是朋友的人,也可能是由神的天使所裝扮而成,而且他們帶來了禮物,一份讓我們在忍耐、理解和寬恕中成長,並讓我們有機會「成為真正的自己」的禮物。

其實,這個寓言第一次是出現在成人書《與神對話》(方智出版)當中,形式與這本書有點兒不同,但同時,它也已經在我受邀演講的大城小鎮傳了開來。我重新創作這個寓言,讓它變成有彩色插畫的童書,以回應無數寫信給我,或是在我演講完後攔住我的人所提供的意見:「它可以成就一個完美的兒童故事。」

我相信,這個寓言是神直接授意的。此外我還知道,任何一個瞭解這個故事的孩子都會因此獲得祝福。感謝你們那麼喜愛孩子,帶領他們來到這個故事當中。

國家圖書館出版品預行編目資料

小靈魂與太陽 / 尼爾‧唐納‧沃許（Neale Donald Walsch）著；劉美欽譯.
-- 初版. -- 臺北市：方智，2014.01
　　72面；14.8×20.8公分 -- （心靈徒步區系列；42）
　　中英雙語版
譯自：The little soul and the sun

ISBN 978-986-175-337-9（平裝）

874.59　　　　　　　　　　　　　　　102023586

The Eurasian Publishing Group
圓神出版事業機構
用心與你對話‧視野無限寬廣　　　方智出版社
Fine Press

http://www.booklife.com.tw　　　　reader@mail.eurasian.com.tw

心靈徒步區系列 042

小靈魂與太陽（中英雙語版）

作　　者／尼爾‧唐納‧沃許（Neale Donald Walsch）
譯　　者／劉美欽
發 行 人／簡志忠
出 版 者／方智出版社股份有限公司
地　　址／台北市南京東路四段50號6樓之1
電　　話／（02）2579-6600‧2579-8800‧2570-3939
傳　　真／（02）2579-0338‧2577-3220‧2570-3636
郵撥帳號／ 13633081　方智出版社股份有限公司
總 編 輯／陳秋月
資深主編／賴良珠
責任編輯／蔡易伶
美術編輯／李　寧
行銷企畫／吳幸芳‧涂姿宇
印務統籌／林永潔
監　　印／高榮祥
校　　對／柳怡如
排　　版／莊寶鈴
經 銷 商／叩應股份有限公司
法律顧問／圓神出版事業機構法律顧問　蕭雄淋律師
印　　刷／國碩印前科技股份有限公司
2014年1月　初版
2023年8月　10刷

The Little Soul and The Sun by Neale Donald Walsch and illustrated by Frank Riccio
Complex Chinese copyright © 2001
by The Eurasian Publishing Group (imprint: Fine Press)
Published by Hampton Roads Publishing Co., Inc. arrangement with Biagi Rights
Management through Andrew Nurnberg Associates International Ltd.
All Rights Reserved.

定價 230 元　　　　　ISBN 978-986-175-337-9

Dear Parents,
and All Lovers of Children:

This wonderful story gives children a new way of looking at why "bad" things sometimes happen, and a new way of dealing with those things when they occur.

The story also teaches that it is very okay to consider yourself special, and to let others know just how special we all are.

Finally, the story shows that everyone is loved by God in the same way, and that even people we may not consider to be our friends may be God's angels in disguise, sent to us to bring us a gift—the gift of growing in tolerance and understanding and forgiveness, and a chance to be who we really are.

This parable first appeared in a slightly different form in the adult book *Conversations with God, Book I*, and has been retold in cities across the country where I have been invited to lecture or offer pulpit talks at church services. I have re-created it as a children's book with color illustrations in response to the comment of countless people who have written to me, or stopped me after my talk, to say that it would "make a perfect children's story."

I believe this parable came directly from God, and I know that any child who becomes familiar with it will be blessed by it. Thank you for loving children enough to bring them this story.

And so, the agreement was made. And the Little Soul went forth into a new lifetime, excited to be the Light, which was very special, and excited to be that part of *special* called Forgiveness.

And the Little Soul waited anxiously to be able to experience itself as Forgiveness, and to thank whatever other soul made it possible.

And at all the moments in that new lifetime, whenever a new soul appeared on the scene, whether that new soul brought joy or sadness—and *especially* if it brought sadness—the Little Soul thought of what God had said.

"Always remember," God had smiled, "I have sent you nothing but angels."

"Good," said the Friendly Soul, "because, you see, I will have been pretending so hard, I will have forgotten myself. And if you do not remember me as I really am, I may not be able to remember for a very long time. And if I forget Who I Am, you may even forget Who You Are, and we will both be lost. Then we will need another soul to come along and remind us both of Who We Are."

"No, we won't!" the Little Soul promised again. "I will remember you! And I will thank you for bringing me this gift—the chance to experience myself as Who I Am."

"Of course this Friendly Soul is an angel!" God interrupted. "Everyone is! Always remember: I have sent you nothing but angels."

And so the Little Soul wanted more than ever to grant the Friendly Soul's request. "What can I do for you?" the Little Soul asked again.

"In the moment that I strike you and smite you," the Friendly Soul replied, "in the moment that I do the worst to you that you could possibly imagine—in that very moment..."

"Yes?" the Little Soul interrupted, "yes...?"

The Friendly Soul became quieter still.

"Remember Who I Really Am."

"Oh, I will!" cried the Little Soul, "I promise! I will always remember you as I see you right here, right now!"

"But what will you do?" the Little Soul asked, just a little nervously, "that will be so terrible?"

"Oh," replied the Friendly Soul with a twinkle, "we'll think of something."

Then the Friendly Soul seemed to turn serious, and said in a quiet voice, "You are right about one thing, you know."

"What is that?" the Little Soul wanted to know.

"I will have to slow down my vibration and become very heavy to do this not-so-nice thing. I will have to pretend to be something very unlike myself. And so, I have but one favor to ask of you in return."

"Oh, anything, anything!" cried the Little Soul, and began to dance and sing, "I get to be forgiving, I get to be forgiving!" Then the Little Soul saw that the Friendly Soul was remaining very quiet.

"What is it?" the Little Soul asked. "What can I do for you? You are such an angel to be willing to do this for me!"

The Little Soul seemed surprised at the answer.

"Don't be so amazed," said the Friendly Soul, "you have done the same thing for me. Don't you remember? Oh, we have danced together, you and I, many times. Through the eons and across all the ages have we danced. Across all time and in many places have we played together. You just don't remember.

"We have both been All Of It. We have been the Up and the Down of it, the Left and the Right of it. We have been the Here and the There of it, the Now and the Then of it. We have been the male and the female, the good and the bad— we have both been the victim and the villain of it.

"Thus have we come together, you and I, many times before; *each* bringing to the *other* the exact and perfect opportunity to Express and to Experience Who We Really Are.

"And so," the Friendly Soul explained a little further, "I will come into your next lifetime and be the 'bad one' this time. I will do something really terrible, and then you can experience yourself as the One Who Forgives."

"But why? Why would you do that?" the Little Soul asked. "You, who are a Being of such utter perfection! You, who vibrate with such a speed that it creates a Light so bright that I can hardly gaze upon you! What could cause you to want to slow down your vibration to such a speed that your bright Light would become dark and dense? What could cause you—who are so light that you dance upon the stars and move throughout the Kingdom with the speed of your thought—to come into my life and make yourself so heavy that you could do this bad thing?"

"Simple," the Friendly Soul said. "I would do it because I love you."

It was then that the Little Soul realized a large crowd had gathered. Souls had come from far and wide—from all over the Kingdom—for the word had gone forth that the Little Soul was having this extraordinary conversation with God, and everyone wanted to hear what they were saying.

Looking at the countless other souls gathered there, the Little Soul had to agree. None appeared less wonderful, less magnificent, or less perfect than the Little Soul itself. Such was the wonder of the souls gathered around, and so bright was their Light, that the Little Soul could scarcely gaze upon them.

"Who, then, to forgive?" asked God.

"Boy, this is going to be no fun at all!" grumbled the Little Soul. "I wanted to experience myself as One Who Forgives. I wanted to know what that part of *special* felt like."

And the Little Soul learned what it must feel like to be sad.

But just then a Friendly Soul stepped forward from the crowd. "Not to worry, Little Soul," the Friendly Soul said, "I will help you."

"You will?" the Little Soul brightened. "But what can you do?"

"Why, I can give you someone to forgive!"

"You can?"

"Certainly!" chirped the Friendly Soul. "I can come into your next lifetime and do something for you to forgive."

"I know what I want to be, I know what I want to be!" the Little Soul announced with great excitement. "I want to be the part of *special* called 'forgiving.' Isn't it special to be forgiving?"

"Oh, yes," God assured the Little Soul. "That is very special."

"Okay," said the Little Soul. "That's what I want to be. I want to be forgiving. I want to experience myself as that."

"Good," said God, "but there's one thing you should know."

The Little Soul was becoming a bit impatient now. It always seemed as though there were some complication.

"What is it?" the Little Soul sighed.

"There is no one to forgive."

"No one?" The Little Soul could hardly believe what had been said.

"No one!" God repeated. "Everything I have made is perfect. There is not a single soul in all creation less perfect than you. Look around you."

"What part of *special*?" the Little Soul repeated. "I don't understand."

"Well," God explained, "being the Light is being special, and being special has a lot of parts to it. It is special to be kind. It is special to be gentle. It is special to be creative. It is special to be patient. Can you think of any other ways it is special to be?" The Little Soul sat quietly for a moment. "I can think of lots of ways to be special!" the Little Soul then exclaimed. "It is special to be helpful. It is special to be sharing. It is special to be friendly. It is special to be considerate of others!"

"Yes!" God agreed, "and you can be all of those things, or any part of *special* you wish to be, at any moment. That's what it means to be the Light."

"Rather be a Light unto the darkness, and don't be mad about it. Then you will know Who You Really Are, and all others will know, too. Let your Light so shine that everyone will know how special you are!"

"You mean it's okay to let others see how special I am?" asked the Little Soul.

"Of course!" God chuckled. "It's very okay! But remember, 'special' does not mean 'better.' Everybody is special, each in their own way! Yet many others have forgotten that. They will see that it is okay for them to be special only when you see that it is okay for you to be special."

"Wow," said the Little Soul, dancing and skipping and laughing and jumping with joy. "I can be as special as I want to be!"

"Yes, and you can start right now," said God, who was dancing and skipping and laughing right along with the Little Soul. "What part of *special* do you want to be?"

"What's darkness?" the Little Soul asked.

God replied, "It is that which you are not."

"Will I be afraid of the dark?" cried the Little Soul.

"Only if you choose to be," God answered. "There is nothing, really, to be afraid of, unless you decide that there is. You see, we are making it all up. We are pretending."

"Oh," said the Little Soul, and felt better already.

Then God explained that, in order to experience anything at all, the exact opposite of it will appear. "It is a great gift," God said, "because without it, you could not know what anything is like.

"You could not know Warm without Cold, Up without Down, Fast without Slow. You could not know Left without Right, Here without There, Now without Then.

"And so," God concluded, "when you are surrounded with darkness, do not shake your fist and raise your voice and curse the darkness.

"Nay, it would be a sun without one of its candles...and that would not be the Sun at all; for it would not shine as brightly. Yet, how to know yourself as the Light when you are *amidst* the Light—that is the question."

"Well," the Little Soul perked up, "you're God. Think of something!"

Once more God smiled. "I already have," God said. "Since you cannot see yourself as the Light when you are *in* the Light, we'll surround you with darkness."

"Well, there is nothing else *but* the Light. You see, I created nothing but what you are; and so, there is no easy way for you to experience yourself as Who You Are, since there is nothing that you are not."

"Huh?" said the Little Soul, who was now a little confused.

"Think of it this way," said God. "You are like a candle in the Sun. Oh, you're there all right. Along with a million, ka-gillion other candles who make up the Sun. And the sun would not be the Sun without you.

But soon, knowing who it was was not enough. The Little Soul felt stirrings inside, and now wanted to *be* who it was. And so the Little Soul went back to God (which is not a bad idea for all souls who want to be Who They Really Are) and said, "Hi, God! Now that I know Who I Am, is it okay for me to be it?"

And God said, "You mean you want to be Who You *Already Are?*"

"Well," replied the Little Soul, "it's one thing to know Who I Am, and another thing altogether to actually be it. I want to feel what it's like to *be* the Light!"

"But you already *are* the Light," God repeated, smiling again.

"Yes, but I want to see what that *feels* like!" cried the Little Soul.

"Well," said God with a chuckle, "I suppose I should have known. You always were the adventuresome one." Then God's expression changed. "There's only one thing..."

"What?" asked the Little Soul.

ONCE UPON NO TIME there was a Little
Soul who said to God, "I know who I am!"

And God said, "That's wonderful! Who are you?"

And the Little Soul shouted, "I'm the Light!"

God smiled a big smile. "That's right!" God exclaimed.
"You are the Light."

The Little Soul was so happy, for it had figured out what
all the souls in the Kingdom were there to figure out. "Wow,"
said the Little Soul, "this is really cool!"

To my future grandchildren,
should there be any,
and to every Little Soul
awaiting birth.

You are our blessing
and our hope,
our innocence
and our joy,
our promise
and our evidence
of God's unending love.

———N.D.W.

To the Blinding Light

———F.R.

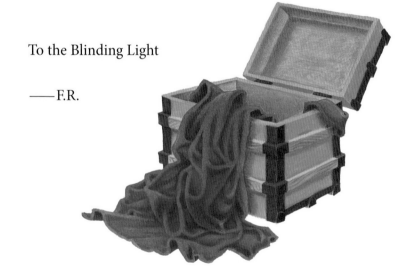

The Little Soul
and the Sun

小靈魂與太陽

（中英雙語版）

Neale Donald Walsch

Illustrated by Frank Riccio

"I can be as special as I want to be!"

the Little Soul shouted,
"I'm the Light!"

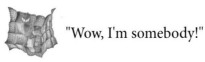"Wow, I'm somebody!"

"I would do it
because I love you."